King Lear

Written by William Shakespeare
Retold by Martin Howard
Illustrated by Rosalind Lyons

Collins

Cast of characters

King Lear

Goneril: King Lear's eldest daughter

Duke of Albany: Goneril's husband

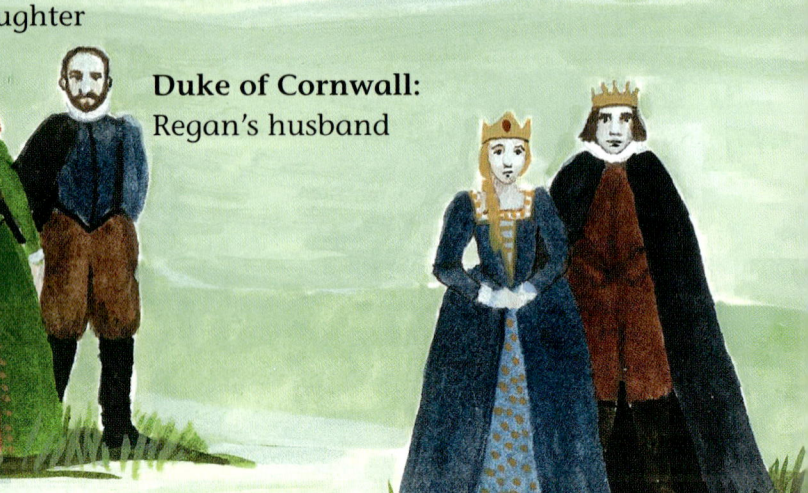

Regan: King Lear's middle daughter

Duke of Cornwall: Regan's husband

Cordelia: King Lear's youngest daughter

King of France: Cordelia's fiancé

1 King Lear

Once, I was a king, powerful and wise and loved by my people. For many years, I sat upon my throne until my hair grew white and my crown heavy. By the time this story began, I was old and tired. But I'd found a way to pass my old age in peace. While I rested my bones, the cares of running a kingdom would pass to my three daughters. Young and full of life, they could rule Britain while I spent a part of the year with each of them in turn: a happy old man surrounded by his family.

What an idiot I was. I should've seen that my dream would be destroyed by greed and jealousy.

It began on a glorious summer day. I sent servants to fetch my daughters and looked out through tall windows in grey stone walls while I waited. Outside, bright flags fluttered from the battlements. Clouds drifted across a blue sky. It was a good day to put aside my worries, I told myself. After I'd spoken to my daughters, I'd go hunting. Stroking my beard, I nodded to myself and looked down as the three girls entered the throne room and stood before me.

The eldest was Goneril. Tall and slim, with a serious face, dark curls fell down her back. She stood stiffly next to her husband, the Duke of Albany.

Regan was shorter, with red hair under her princess's gold crown. Both she and the Duke of Cornwall, her husband, had a crafty look in their eyes. They'd make wise rulers, I told myself.

The youngest – Cordelia – had lighter hair and a sweet smile. She didn't seem curious about why I'd summoned her, and watched birds play outside the windows. At her side, the young King of France gazed down at her. The day before, he'd asked for Cordelia's hand in marriage.

"I've decided to step down from the throne," I said loudly.

Even Cordelia looked round at that. Goneril's eyes widened in surprise and Regan opened her mouth to speak. Holding up a hand to stop her, I took a map that my faithful servant, the Earl of Kent, held out to me. It showed Britain divided into three. "My mind's made up. Each of you will have a third of my kingdom to rule ... if you pass my test."

"What test?" Goneril asked, sharply. She'd always been the cleverest of the three.

"A simple test," I said. "All I want is for each of my daughters to tell me how much they love me."

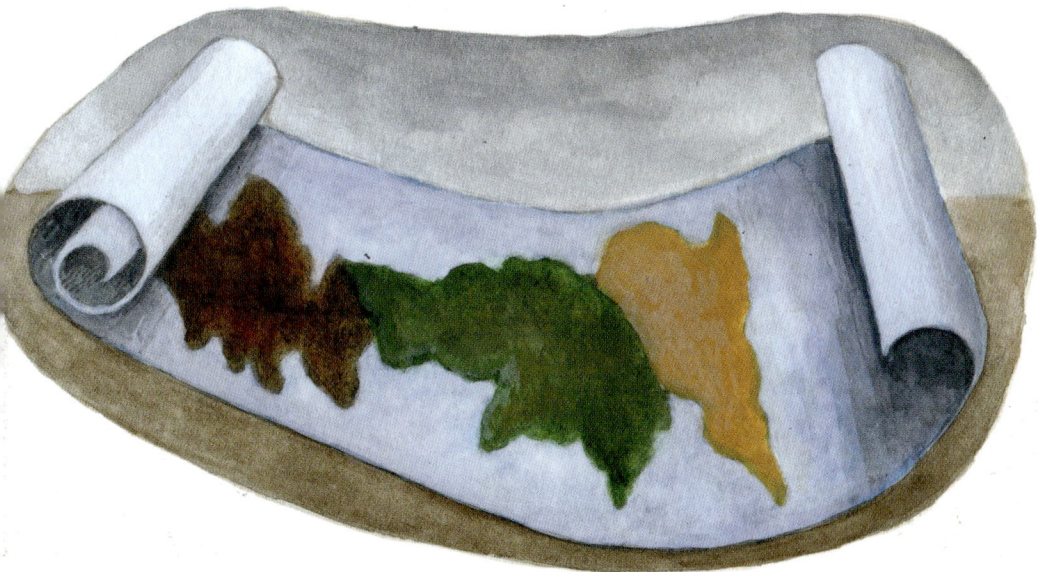

A frown crossed Cordelia's face. I ignored it. "Goneril," I continued, "as the eldest, you'll be the first."

She began quickly. "Father, you're dearer to me than any riches on Earth, dearer than freedom and dearer than my life. Besides you, nothing else in this world means anything to me. I love you more than any child ever loved their parent. The words haven't been invented to show you how deep and truly."

I nodded. Pointing at a section of the map, I said, "I'm pleased with you, Goneril. These will be your lands to rule over."

Then I turned to Regan, who blushed. "My love's like my sister's," she said. "Except that I love you more. My only joy in life is my love for you and all I hope is that my great love might be returned by my noble father."

"It is, Regan," I told her, pointing to the map again. "As proof, I give you lands as large as Goneril's."

At last, I smiled down at Cordelia. "And now it's your turn," I said. "What will you say of your love for me, Cordelia?"

Cordelia frowned again. "Nothing," she said.

"Nothing!" I almost jumped from my throne in shock.

"Nothing," Cordelia said again, sounding annoyed. "This is silly. My sisters don't love you more than anything else in the world, they're just telling you what you want to hear. I'm sure they love you but not just you. They love their husbands too, I hope." Glancing up into the King of France's face, she added, "When I'm married, I'm going to love my husband just as much as I love my father."

My face reddened with anger. "I always loved you the most, Cordelia. How could you be so cruel," I growled.

Cordelia shrugged. "It's the truth," she said. "Of course I love you, as any daughter loves her father, but I won't take part in this ridiculous flattery."

"Flattery!" I shouted, glaring and pointing a shaking finger at her. "If you love truth so much then truth will be all you have. Get out of my sight."

"My lord," the Earl of Kent gasped, "she's just speaking honestly, and she's your daughter – "

"I suppose you think I'm just a ridiculous old man looking for flattery, too, Kent!" I yelled at him. "Well, she's no daughter of mine, and you can get out with her."

Taking the map, I ripped it into shreds. "Both of you are exiled. Britain will be shared between the two daughters who do love me. The third can go and live in France if the French king will still marry her with no land, no money and no jewels."

"I'll marry Cordelia and count myself the luckiest man on Earth," said the King of France with a cold bow. "Your daughter's worth more than any riches." Taking the shocked Cordelia's hand, he led her away. As they reached the great wooden doors, she looked over her shoulder and called back to her sisters, "Look after our father."

In reply, Goneril and Regan sneered and turned their backs.

2 Edmund

That wrinkled old idiot King Lear was about to be betrayed by two of his own daughters. Good for Goneril and Regan, I say. Clever women. But Lear wasn't the only doddering grey-haired twit about to get tricked. My name's Edmund, the younger son of the Duke of Gloucester, one of the king's oldest friends, and almost as rich. I, too, was about to betray my family. Some might call that wicked, but I say you have to look out for yourself in this world – especially when you have a noble and handsome older brother everyone loves more than you.

Edgar. How I hated him. My brother was the sort of man who believes in goodness and justice and all that rubbish. I pretended to like him, but really he made me want to throw up. And just because he was older than me, my father's land and money and power would go to him when the old man died. It was unfair. Why should that man get everything just because he was older than me? So I made a plan to take what I deserved.

It was easy. I knew my brother's handwriting well enough to fake it, so I wrote a letter and signed his name at the bottom. My father had been at King Lear's castle when Lear was giving his throne away. When he returned, I made sure the letter was in my hand as he entered the great hall of our home. As usual, the silly old twerp was moaning.

"Terrible news, Edmund. The Earl of Kent's been banished from Britain. Princess Cordelia too. The King of France is furious." Shaking his head sadly, he gave me a hug. "What's your news, my son?"

"I've no news, Father," I replied, pretending to hide the letter.

"Of course you have news. What's that?"

"Nothing … It's nothing," I screwed it up.

"Is it a love letter? Let me see." Chuckling, he snatched the paper from my hand.

"No, Father," I said, making my voice sound horrified and pretending to grab at the letter.

My father ignored me. "My dear brother Edmund," he read aloud. "I wish to speak to you about a matter of great importance. I would like to inherit father's title and lands before I'm too old to enjoy them, but the old man shows no sign of dying. If you and I could find some way to stop him living so long, then I'd gladly share all I inherit. Your brother, Edgar."

While he read, my father's face went pale. By the time he finished, his voice was a whisper and he was shaking. "He wants to murder me," he croaked. "My own son! It can't be true, but it's his handwriting." He turned to glare at me. "Are you plotting with him?"

"Of course not!" I pretended to be outraged. "I didn't want you to see the letter because I'm certain it's a fake. Edgar's so good and kind that someone must be trying to cause trouble. Wait here, I'll go and find him. I'm sure there must be an explanation."

I hurried away. Edgar had no idea about the letter, of course. I'd written it, and now I wanted to make my dumb older brother look even guiltier. I found him in the stable, grooming his horse. Seeing me run in, he grinned. "Edmund! Do you want to come riding with me …" The smile left his face as he saw my expression. "What's the matter?" he asked. "What's happened?"

"It's Father," I said. "He's in a terrible rage with you. You must get out of the castle at once before he finds you."

"But why is he angry with me? I haven't done anything to upset him." Confusion spread across Edgar's stupid face. "I'd better go and see him so we can get to the bottom of this."

"No!" I shouted. "I'm sure it's just a misunderstanding, but he's too angry to listen to anyone right now, especially you. Until he calms down you'd better hide. I can hear him coming. Go – fast!"

Edgar scrambled on to his horse. Looking down at me, he said, "Will you come and find me when his rage has passed?"

"Of course, Brother," I told him, slapping the horse's rump. "You can count on me."

As Edgar's horse clattered out of the stable at a gallop, I heard my father shouting from the courtyard. "Stop, you villain. STOP!"

The old man thought Edgar was running away because his letter had been discovered. It was brilliant! Only one thing could make Edgar look even guiltier.

Pulling my sword from its sheath, I stabbed myself in the arm, and stumbled out. Blood oozed between my fingers where I held the wound.

"I tried to stop him, Father," I yelled, "but he tried to kill me."

Red-faced with fury, my father called for guards and sent them after poor, confused, stupid Edgar. "From this day forwards, Edmund, you're my only son," he said, throwing an arm around my shoulder. "If Edgar ever tries to return, he'll pay for this with his life."

I couldn't help it – I grinned. Now no one stood between me and my father's wealth. My plan had worked beautifully.

3 The fool

I may have been a fool, dressed in bells and a silly hat, but it was my master, King Lear, who was the truly foolish man. He gave away his kingdom and sent away the daughter who loved him, and the Earl of Kent, his most loyal servant. It was a terrible mistake and, by the time a few weeks had passed, my smile had gone and my jokes had lost their punchlines. Every hour brought more arguments. As soon as her father stepped down from the throne, Goneril began turning the whole palace against anyone who remained loyal to her father.

Lear watched everything she did to make sure she ruled Britain well, and she hated it. She wanted to get rid of all his soldiers and servants so he'd be alone and powerless. Then, she could rule however she liked. I told my king a hundred times to beware of his daughter, but he wouldn't listen – until this morning.

Oh my bells! This morning, disaster fell.

A man arrived, dressed in rags with a straggly beard. He said his name was Caius and that he was looking for a job as a servant to the king. The king didn't recognise him, but I saw at once that it was the Earl of Kent in disguise.

I said nothing to the king though. I knew Kent had come to try and protect him from Goneril, and Lear would only send him away again, or worse, if he knew who he really was.

Kent soon proved that I was right.

Like I said, Goneril had turned the palace against us. When the king asked a servant where Goneril was, the servant just shrugged. "My lady's busy and doesn't wish to see you," he said with a sneer.

Kent pushed him so hard he sprawled on the floor. "How dare you speak to your king like that!" he yelled.

For the first time since we'd arrived at Goneril's palace, I grinned. "I like this new servant," I told the king. Turning to Kent, I offered him my hat. Its bells tinkled. "Here," I said. "Take my crown. Fools and kings and foolish kings always give theirs away."

"Call me a fool! I'll have you beaten!" King Lear growled.

"Now I can see you're truly your daughter's father," I replied with a sad jingle. "But she had me beaten yesterday for being loyal to you. You'll have me beaten for being disloyal to you."

Before my king could reply, Goneril marched down the stone staircase, shouting, "Father, what's the meaning of this?"

"Your servant – "

Goneril interrupted him by poking him in the chest. "My servants," she spat. "What about your servants? All they do is cause trouble."

Looking at the two of them glaring angrily at each other, I thought it might be a good time for a joke. Just to lighten the mood. I'm a fool after all. "I say, I say, I say," I said, with a jingle of my bells, "have you heard the one about the cuckoo who had his head bitten off by his own chick?"

"Quiet!" shouted Goneril. I guess she didn't have a very good sense of humour. Poking her father again, she said, "Even your fool makes trouble. What do you need so many servants for anyway? You're not a king any more, just a silly old man."

A look of shock spread across Lear's face. "Saddle my horse," he shouted. "I'd rather be bitten by snakes than stay another night here. Luckily, I have another daughter. Regan will welcome me even if you're a heartless monster, Goneril, and you'll find that I'm still a king – a king who isn't too old to fight his enemies."

Goneril turned to me with a snarl. "You can get out, too," she said. "Follow your feeble old master. I'll make sure he doesn't find a welcome with my sister."

As I scurried out of the palace, I saw the king ahead of me, sitting on a rearing horse. "You," he commanded, pointing to Kent, "ride ahead as fast as you can and tell Regan I'm coming."

4 Goneril

My grip on Britain was growing stronger. Everything was going so well, I could've kissed myself. After my idiot father scurried away with his soldiers and that infuriating fool, I returned to my room. There, I wrote a letter to my sister. My father thought she'd take his side but Regan would do as I told her. I needed her to help to bring our father under our control so I told her to leave her castle and go to the Duke of Gloucester's. If she wasn't at home, I wrote, she couldn't be expected to let Father stay with her, along with all his knights and servants. He'd be homeless. That would teach the old fool a lesson.

We ruled Britain, not him. The last thing we needed was our father looking over our shoulders all the time, especially when he had 100 armed knights ready for battle if we disobeyed him. So, I told her my plans and wrote that I'd be arriving soon. Then, I sent the letter ahead with a servant on a fast horse.

When I reached the Duke of Gloucester's castle a few days later, I galloped across the drawbridge to find a small crowd gathered in the courtyard outside the castle doors. A ragged man I recognised as my father's new servant – Caius, I think his name was – had been put in the stocks and was looking very sorry for himself. A good start, I smiled to myself. Regan had obviously read my letter.

My father had arrived just before me. He was still sitting on his horse, shouting at Regan while Regan's husband Cornwall stood gawping along with the Duke of Gloucester and his handsome son Edmund. I pulled on my horse's reins and trotted over. "What's going on here?" I asked as I reached the group and dismounted.

"Goneril!" Regan shouted, pointing a furious finger at Caius. "This stinking, low-born servant of Father's attacked the messenger you sent. It's an outrage! I had to punish him."

"He's the same servant I hit at your castle," Caius yelled from the stocks. "A sneaky traitor to the king, and a coward."

Of course, I ignored him. "You've given him the punishment he deserves, Sister," I told Regan. "We had the same problem with father's servants at my palace. They're all troublemakers."

"It's a crime to treat the king's men like this," said Gloucester. "If he's done wrong then the king and the king alone should punish him."

"Silence," I commanded. "My sister and I rule this kingdom. We'll deal with this."

"Goneril," my father snarled. "Aren't you ashamed of yourself?" Turning to Regan, he said, "And you, Regan? I came to you for help. Are you going to take your sister's side against your own father?"

In the distance thunder rumbled.

Regan smiled sweetly. "But Goneril's right, Father," she said. "You're old and your men do nothing except cause trouble. Why do you need so many anyway? Send half of them away and apologise to Goneril. Then you can return to her palace. I can't take you in."

Father's face went red.

Before he could reply, I said, "Half of them, Regan? But that would leave 50 men. An old man doesn't need 50 soldiers. Surely, 25 would be enough?"

"You're right, Goneril," Regan replied.

"I think I am, Sister," I said with a smile. "But really, why does he need 25, or ten, or five? My palace is already full of servants and soldiers."

"Hmmm ... perhaps even one would be too many," said Regan.

Thunder rumbled again, and lightning crackled over the horizon. From the dark clouds above rain began to lash down.

Raising his voice my father howled, "You think that because I'm old I'm stupid, but I see into your hearts. I loved you. I gave you my throne. And in return, you plot to throw me out like kitchen scraps. My heart breaks to have two traitors as daughters." Raindrops and tears rolled down his cheeks. As thunder crashed again, his horse reared, its hooves pawing at the air. And still my father roared. "You're no daughters of mine. You're cruel, power-hungry hags whose selfish ingratitude will send me mad with grief."

Sobbing, he pulled his horse around. Hooves clattered on the wooden drawbridge as he galloped into the storm, his cloak billowing out behind him.

With a cry of "Hoy, wait for me", his ridiculous fool followed him.

For a few moments, the only sounds were the beating of rain on the cobblestones, and the growl of thunder.

Gloucester was the first to speak. He looked horrified. "Night's coming and there's no shelter within miles. We have to stop him."

Regan sniffed. "Lock your castle gates, Gloucester. He'll find no shelter here."

I took Regan's arm. Together we turned back towards the castle. "Quite right, Sister," I said. "If he's silly enough to go riding out into a storm, whatever happens is his own fault." I glanced at Regan. She was staring at Gloucester's son, Edmund. He really was very, very handsome, I thought.

5 Kent

When Goneril and Regan disappeared inside the castle, Gloucester set me free from the stocks. Luckily, he didn't recognise me as the Earl of Kent. Gloucester was a good man and I could see he was troubled by what Goneril and Regan had done. "There are horses in the stable. Take one and go after your master," he said, quickly. "I'll speak to his daughters. Maybe I can bring them to their senses. Go, find him. I'll follow."

I didn't need telling twice. Throwing myself on to a horse, I galloped after the king.

Rain turned the ground into thick mud. The sky grew darker with every mile. Thunder cracked across the sky. But I didn't slow down until I saw a pale face in the darkness: one of the king's men. "Where's the king?" I shouted.

The man looked frightened. "Gone into the storm with the fool," he said. "I think his daughters' betrayal has driven him mad."

I kicked my horse onwards, galloping through sheets of rain and never-ending thunder. I passed a hut. It was tiny and made of mud, but it would be dry inside. If I could just find the king, we could shelter there.

A few minutes later, I galloped into a scene from a nightmare. King Lear stood in the middle of the moor, his arms wide. Wind blew through his soaked clothes and white hair. Lightning crackled. The fool danced around, trying to distract him with jokes and songs. It did no good. The king had gone mad. "Blow wind," he screamed into the hurricane. "Do your worst. Spit fire and rain at me and destroy all of us. Me, my ungrateful daughters, and my kingdom. I don't care. I'm weak and old and even my own children hate me."

The fool jigged around him, but the king was lost in despair. Throwing back his head, he howled at the black clouds above.

Someone had to bring him to his senses. I shouted, "My king. In all my life, I've never seen such a terrible storm. We must find shelter!"

King Lear laughed. "Shelter?" he bellowed. "Why would I want to shelter from this storm? The storm's my friend. The storm will wash us all away and make Britain clean again."

There was nothing else for it. The king was mad. I would have to drag him to shelter. Throwing myself from my horse into ankle-deep mud, I stumbled towards him. Wind and rain battered my face.

The king groaned as I took his arm. "How could they do it?" he sobbed. "How could they betray me? My beloved daughters …"

I said nothing. The fool grabbed his other arm and together we pulled him towards the hut.

6 Edmund

I've had the most amazing stroke of luck! With my brainless maggot of a brother, Edgar, out of the way, I needed to get rid of my father, too. I couldn't become the Duke of Gloucester while he was still around. But I couldn't think of any way to remove him. Tonight though, a plan just fell into my hands. And it was my father who gave it to me!

A storm was raging outside, banging the doors and windows, when my father came out of a room where he'd been talking to Goneril and Regan. He held a flickering candle that lit his pale face. "Oh, Edmund. This is dreadful," he said.

"What?" I asked.

"I hoped that Regan and Goneril would make peace with their father," he groaned. "But they told me to mind my own business. And the storm's terrible. The king will die out there, but I'm not allowed to help him."

"Oh," I said, pretending to care. "Yes. Terrible. Children should be kind to their parents and all that."

"But the king's my friend and I've important news for him. Regan and Goneril will punish me but I must go after him."

Suddenly I was interested. I liked the idea of my father being punished. "What news?" I asked, quickly.

"A letter arrived earlier, from Cordelia," he said. "She's in Dover with the French army. She's going to march across Britain and take the country back for her father."

I almost gasped. This was treachery! Goneril and Regan would be furious with my father if they knew he was plotting with Cordelia. "Where's the letter?" I asked.

"In a drawer in my room," my father told me. "Edmund, we're in a dangerous situation, but I trust you. Regan and Goneril mustn't know that I've followed the king. I'll slip out of the castle quietly. Tell them I'm ill. Tell them I've gone to bed."

"Of course. Of course," I said, as he hurried away along the stone corridor. I couldn't believe my luck. My father really was the most brainless old idiot. I'd find the letter and, as soon as he was gone, I'd show it to Regan and Goneril. He'd be banished. They might even have him killed. And I'd be rewarded.

Edmund, Duke of Gloucester. It sounded good!

7 Lear

My fool and my new servant, Caius, brought me to a small hut in the middle of the moor. The windows rattled as the storm raged outside, but the storm in my own mind was worse. I should've been sitting by the fire with a feast, or warm in my royal bed. Instead, Regan and Goneril were pushing me out of the kingdom I'd given them. I was miserable, wet and cold, in a freezing hut with only a fool and a servant I hardly knew for company.

They thought I'd gone mad. They were right: I had. Who wouldn't have been driven mad by two such evil, ungrateful daughters? There's nothing worse in the world than to be betrayed by your own children. Tears ran down my face when I remembered how cold and cruel I'd been to my old friend Kent, and to Cordelia. Poor Cordelia. She'd been honest with me and I'd thrown her out of her home. Kent had tried to warn me. What a stupid, awful idiot I'd been. I deserved to suffer, I told myself.

Shaking with cold on the mud floor, I wrapped my arms around myself. Hours passed and I wished I was dead.

In the middle of the night the door crashed open. The Duke of Gloucester stood in the doorway, holding up a fiery torch. "My king, I've found you!" he cried. "I've news. Important news!"

I didn't answer. His news didn't matter to me. I didn't care.

"Don't trouble him with news, sir," said Caius. "He's mad with grief already."

Gloucester looked down at me. "I'm not surprised," he said. "I know how he must feel. My own son, Edgar, plotted to kill me ..."

"Children," I muttered. "They're poisonous snakes. Biting dogs, with hearts made of stone." Shivering, I rocked backwards and forwards.

"You see, my lord Gloucester, he talks nonsense," said Caius, shaking his head.

"I disobeyed his daughters," Gloucester told him. "Outside is a cart with warm clothes and food. Take the king to Dover. Cordelia's there with the French king and his army. He must go quickly."

A small flicker of hope stirred, and died again. I groaned to myself. How could I face my sweet Cordelia after what I'd said to her? I put my head in my hands and sobbed.

Caius jumped up. "This is excellent news, my lord," he shouted. Turning to the fool, he said, "Help me carry the king. We're going to Dover."

"And I must get back to my castle before Goneril and Regan find out I'm missing," said Gloucester. Opening the door, he bowed to me and then he was gone into the wind and thunder.

8 Gloucester

Guards grabbed me as soon as I set foot through the castle gate. I was chained and marched to the great hall. Lit by blazing torches, Goneril, Regan and Cornwall were waiting for me.

At their side was Edmund. He grinned at me as I was pushed to my knees on the cold stone floor. In Goneril's hand was the letter from Cordelia.

My son had betrayed me.

As soon as I saw his smug face, I knew he'd done the same to his brother. I should've known, I told myself angrily. Edgar was always so good and kind. He would never have plotted against me. It'd been Edmund all along.

A groan escaped my lips.

"Traitor!" Goneril spat the word out.

Cornwall held up a hand. Firelight flickered across his spiteful face. "Wait," he interrupted. Turning to Edmund, he said, "You're the Duke of Gloucester now and there's work to be done. The French could attack at any moment. Goneril's leaving to gather an army. After we've dealt with your father, you must go with her."

I shuddered at his words. Edmund's betrayal meant that Goneril and Regan would have time to gather their forces before the French attacked. With a sneer, Cornwall kicked me. Regan snatched my beard and pulled out a handful of hair. "Disgusting traitor," she said with a snarl. "Where's my mad father?"

"On his way to Dover," I told her. "Yes, I betrayed you and I'm glad I did. I'll see him revenged against his vicious daughters."

"You'll see nothing!" Cornwall shouted angrily, drawing a dagger and lunging at me.

A second later I was blind and in terrible pain. With a scream of agony and confusion, I clutched my face and felt blood trickle between my fingers.

"No! Leave my master alone!"

Even in my pain I recognised the voice. It belonged to one of my servants: a boy I'd always liked. Everything was black but I heard the metal sound of a sword being pulled from its sheath. Cornwall yelled.

"You've killed him!" Regan screamed. "You murdered my husband! I'll have your life, too."

Another scream echoed around the great hall. A body fell beside me. My young servant. I stretched out a hand and felt his lifeless face. Regan had killed him!

For a few moments there was silence, except the sound of Regan panting and my own sobs of agony. Then she said, "Guards, take the traitor. Throw him out, like the rubbish he is."

Hands grabbed at me. Terrified, I was pushed along corridors until rain and wind hit my face. Then I was shoved into the mud, moaning and clutching my sightless eyes. The massive doors of my castle slammed behind me.

I could do nothing but sob as the rain poured down on me. My whole world had turned dark. I had lost my sons, my castle and my eyes. I don't know how long I lay in the mud but it felt like hours until, finally, a hand reached for my shoulder.

"What? Who's there? Who are you?" I asked. My voice was a croak.

"Just a beggar," replied a young man's voice. "A poor beggar who wanders the roads. You can call me Mad Tom. Can I help you, master?"

"Yes, you can help me, Mad Tom," I replied, staggering to my feet with his help. "I've lost one son and been betrayed by another. My king's mad and Britain's ruled by his wicked daughters. There's nothing left in this life for me. Lead me to the great cliffs of Dover so I can throw myself off."

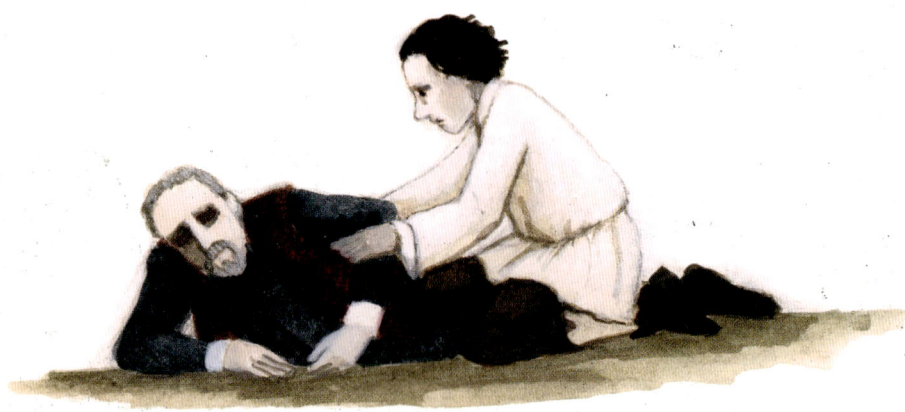

9 Goneril

What a difference there can be between two men. Together, Edmund, the new Duke of Gloucester, and I rode through Britain, raising an army. He was handsome and brave and loyal. I couldn't help comparing him to my cowardly, pathetic husband.

By the time Edmund returned to his castle and I went back to my palace, I was sure that he'd make a far better husband for me than Albany. When I got home all I heard was Albany whining, "Goneril, you've become a monster," and "Goneril, Edmund's betrayal of his own father was a disgusting crime."

The only crime was that I'd married a whimpering dog. The French army had arrived in Dover and all my ridiculous husband could do was complain about how heartless I'd become. But I'm not heartless and my heart told me that I wished to be married to Edmund.

If Regan didn't marry him first.

I'd seen the way my sister looked at Edmund when we were at the Duke of Gloucester's castle. She loved him, I was sure. And with her own husband now dead she was free to marry my Edmund. Stupid Regan who just blinded Gloucester and let him go. She should've killed him.

Still, I was queen. I could do whatever I liked, and I swore I'd find a way to get rid of Albany and marry Edmund. I'd fix Regan, too. Then Edmund and I could rule the whole country together. First, I decided to send a letter with a servant on the fastest horse in the stables. Edmund would soon know my plans for him and me.

10 Edgar

My little brother Edmund has done such terrible things I can hardly believe they're true. After I ran away from my father's castle I swore that he would pay for his crimes and disguised myself. Mad Tom, I called myself. Dressed in rags so that no one would know I was really Edgar, the Duke of Gloucester's elder son, I stayed close to the castle. I hoped that I could find out what Edmund was planning and stop him. It was lucky that I was there when my father was kicked out – blind and mad with pain. I helped him out of the mud and led him towards Dover, not so that he could kill himself, but so that he could find safety with Cordelia and the French army. I didn't tell him who I really was. He was in shock already. Another might've killed him.

We walked and stumbled slowly along the road for days until, one morning, a rider stopped his horse suddenly in front of us. "You're the Duke of Gloucester," he said, sounding surprised.

My father groaned. "I'm no longer the Duke of Gloucester," he said. "Just an old, blind man."

The man climbed down from his horse. A sword appeared in his hand. "An old, blind man who'll make me rich," he said. "My mistress, Queen Goneril, was unhappy that her sister let you live. She'll reward me when I tell her that I've corrected Regan's mistake with my own sword."

I stepped in front of my father.

"Get out of the way, stupid beggar," the servant hissed. "This man's a traitor. If you help him then you're a traitor too. I'll kill you both."

"Keep away from him," I said quietly.

Goneril's servant ignored me and lunged forwards with his sword.

Pulling my own blade from where it was hidden beneath my rags, I swept his sword aside with a clash of metal.

He was surprised a beggar could fight. I took advantage of his confusion. Kicking him in the stomach, I forced him back. Our blades cut through the air, crashing against each other again and again as we fought. "But … but … you're just a ragged tramp," he gasped as my blade flashed like lightning. "How can you fight so well?"

The coward would've killed my father – an unarmed blind man. He didn't deserve an answer. Instead, I smiled grimly and thrust my sword at him.

He fell. Blood poured from a wound in his side. "I'm dying," he croaked. "Please, there's a letter in my bag for Edmund, the Duke of Gloucester, from my mistress. Deliver it and you may take the money you'll also find there."

Those were his last words. Closing his eyes, he died.

I found the letter in the saddlebag of his horse. Opening it, I read aloud to my father, "My darling Edmund, I'm overwhelmed with love for you. But my husband, the Duke of Albany, stands between us. If you wish to marry me and become the most powerful man in Britain you must kill him. Tell me you'll do it and I'll arrange a time and a place when he'll be alone, my love." The letter was signed "Your wife (if you'll have me), Goneril."

I shook my head in disgust. Goneril was plotting to kill her own husband, and marry my brother in his place. Was there no crime that was too foul for the two of them?

I helped my father to his feet. "Come on," I said. "Mad Tom will lead you to Dover."

The letter proved that Goneril was an evil, murderous, traitor. The British army would soon be at Dover, and Goneril's husband, the Duke of Albany, would be there, too. He'd know what to do with his wife's letter.

11 Cordelia

The Earl of Kent brought my father back to me. Bless his kind and noble heart. When the two of them, and my father's loyal fool, staggered into my camp at Dover, the king was sick and mad with grief. He muttered constantly about crows and storms.

At first he didn't know me, but I had a warm bed made up for him in my own tent and gave him hot drinks and watched over him while he slept. Finally, when he woke, he looked up at me with tears in his eyes. Reaching out a bony hand, he touched my cheek.

"Oh, my dear father," I said, gently. "What have my sisters done to you?"

"Where am I?" he whispered.

"You're safe now, Father. With me. Do you know who I am?"

Another tear trickled down his cheek. "My daughter, Cordelia," he said, and turned his head away from me. "How you must hate me. Your sisters had no reason, but I've given you every reason to want me dead."

Taking his hand, I kissed it. "You're the king and you did what you thought best, Father," I said. "It's not your fault that Goneril and Regan betrayed you."

Outside a drum began to beat. Kent stepped forwards to stand at my side. "The British army's coming," he said. "Can the king stand? Battle's coming and we must get him to safety."

I felt the blood drain from my face. My husband had returned to France to deal with an urgent matter. He wasn't here to command his army. Regan and Goneril had arrived too soon.

"I can stand if Cordelia will let me lean on her," my father said. "But I won't run. Find me somewhere I can watch the battle."

With a sinking heart, I led my father out of the tent. I'd a terrible feeling that without the French king to command it, his army would be destroyed.

12 Edmund

Everything went better than I could ever have dreamt! Under my command, the British army thundered across the field of battle and destroyed the French. I looked amazing in my brightly polished armour. Trumpets blaring, my British forces rode down upon the French and crushed them while I sat upon my rearing horse, sword held high and glittering in the sunshine. Of course, I didn't get too close to the actual fighting. I'd worked too hard to get where I was to die in some stupid battle. I did shout a lot though. Thankfully, it was a quick battle and no one noticed there was no blood on my sword.

As well as that I captured mad King Lear and Cordelia! A few weeks ago, I was just the younger son of the Duke of Gloucester, now I was putting kings and princesses in chains and having them dragged off to the dungeons! That pathetic worm Albany told me to treat them kindly. I paid no attention to him. Instead, I gave orders to a young captain to make sure they didn't live another day. I mean, who cared about that old idiot and his soppy daughter? Britain belonged to Regan and Goneril, and soon it would belong to me!

My only problem was which one of the sisters to marry. Both of them were madly in love with me and who could blame them? Edmund, Duke of Gloucester: young and handsome and a hero, too! I decided to choose which one to marry carefully. Sooner or later they'd fight each other. Britain would be whole again and, if I married the right sister, I'd be king of it all!

Edmund, King of Britain! It sounded great.

13 Edgar

The Duke of Gloucester, my father, died. His wounds and his sadness at all that'd happened had left him weak. When I told him that the French army had been defeated and Edmund had taken Cordelia and King Lear prisoner, it was too much for him. He stumbled and fell to the ground in horror. There was just time to tell him that I wasn't really Mad Tom the beggar but his own son, Edgar, before he passed away. He begged my forgiveness, and I held him in my arms until his sightless eyes closed for the last time.

It was all my brother's fault! Edmund would pay for his crimes. The world would know what a murderous, disgraceful traitor he was.

I knew exactly what I had to do.

A little later, Edmund returned to camp after taking his prisoners to a dungeon. Waiting for him were Goneril and Regan and the Duke of Albany. Regan looked pale. Edmund got off his horse and bowed to the three of them. He looked extremely pleased with himself.

"Are the king and Cordelia safe?" Albany demanded.

Edmund smiled a sly smile. "They are, my lord," he said. "Safe in a dungeon until it's decided what to do with them."

"I don't believe you. Bring them here," Albany replied.

Edmund scowled. "I'm tired from fighting," he said. "You can see them tomorrow."

With her eyes shining, Regan spoke next. She coughed and said in a weak voice, "Stop this, Albany. Edmund fought bravely today. Britain owes him a reward, and his reward is me. We'll be married. All my titles and wealth will be his, too."

Goneril snarled. "You can't marry him."

"No one's going to marry him!" Albany's angry shout echoed around the camp.

Edmund's grin faded.

Goneril went pale.

Regan stumbled.

"You're nothing but a filthy, dishonourable criminal, Edmund, Duke of Gloucester," Albany continued. His face was red with anger. "I'll have you executed …"

"No!" Goneril interrupted him. She clutched Albany's arm. "Have you gone mad? Stop this!"

Pushing his wife away, Albany drew his sword. "I'll not stop until this disgusting snake's dead," he said.

Regan staggered and fell. She held a hand to her throat. "I'm sick," she croaked.

Even though he was angry, Albany stopped and knelt by her. "She's very ill," he said. "Guards, carry her to my tent and fetch a doctor."

While he was on his knees, I stepped out from behind the tree where I'd been hiding, and stood in front of Edmund. "My Lord Albany," I said in a loud, clear voice, "I can't let you fight this man. Not whilst I'm able to carry a sword."

"I don't fight beggars," Edmund sneered.

"I'm as noble as you," I told him. "And I, too, say you're a criminal. Your betrayal killed your own father."

"I'm no criminal," Edmund growled.

"Then prove it with your sword," I said. My own blade howled through the air.

Edmund dodged and swung back. The air filled with the clash of steel against steel as we cut at each other. "Who are you?" Edmund grunted as he pulled his arm back for a killing blow.

I stepped aside and thrust.

The tip of my sword caught Edmund in the chest. His eyes went wide with shock. A moment later he staggered and fell to the grass.

"Edmund!" Goneril jumped towards my brother. "Guards! Guards! Kill this man," she shouted, pointing at me.

"Guards, don't obey her," Albany shouted. "She's a criminal, too. I've proof in her own words." From his pocket he pulled the letter I'd secretly given to him earlier and threw it at her.

Goneril picked it up and stared at it. Her face went white.

"I see you recognise your own writing," said Albany. "You wanted proof, well here it is. You wanted Edmund to murder me. Queen or not, you'll be hanged for this."

Goneril opened her mouth to speak, but a servant rushed from a tent, shouting, "Murder! Murder! Queen Regan's dead. The doctor says it's poison."

Albany gasped. "You!" he yelled at Goneril. "You've betrayed your father, plotted to kill me and now you've poisoned your own sister to stop her marrying Edmund. Do you deny it?"

"I … I … don't ask me!" Goneril turned to run. Seeing guards closing in on her, she snatched the dagger from Albany's belt instead and plunged it into her own heart.

As I watched her fall to the ground, dead, I felt a hand clutch at my ankle. Edmund was still alive, though only just. Falling to my knees, I looked into his eyes.

"I'm as wicked and guilty as you say I am," he gasped. "And I'm sorry for what I've done. But I would like to know the name of the man who killed me before I die."

Pulling back the hood I was wearing, I replied, "I'm your brother, Edgar, come to take revenge for our father's life."

"I deserve it," sighed Edmund. "I betrayed you and Father, and I would've agreed to marry both Regan and Goneril. I've done terrible things but I can still do one good thing before I die. I ordered Lear and Cordelia's deaths, but it may not be too late to stop …"

Edmund coughed. Closing his eyes, my brother died.

Albany was already on his feet sending guards to release Lear and Cordelia. But he was too late.

Horses galloped towards their prison, but by the time they arrived Cordelia had been hanged in her jail. King Lear had fought to save her but he was too old and weak. He stumbled out of the prison and staggered towards us. In his arms he held Cordelia's body. Tears ran down his cheeks. He howled his grief at the sky and fell to his knees, weeping over Cordelia. "All the sorrows I ever felt are nothing next to this," he sobbed.

14 The fool

So, this is how the story ends – with a sad fool whose bells and laughter have been drowned by tears.
I watched it all, and now it's up to me to end this sorry tale of greed and betrayal. I'll do it quickly or my own tears will smudge the ink from my pen.

While Lear wept over his daughter's body, Kent knelt next to him and laid a hand on his shoulder. "Oh my poor master," he said.

"Get away from me." Lear pushed him away.

"But it's me, Kent. I'm your friend."

"Kent's a traitor. Not like my good servant Caius. Where's Caius?"

King Lear's grief had driven him deeper into madness.

"My king," Albany interrupted with a gentle voice. "Goneril and Regan are dead, too. Someone must rule Britain. For the sake of the country, you must put your grief aside and take the throne again."

"Everyone's dead," groaned Lear. "Never, never, never, shall I sit on that throne again. Look at my sweet Cordelia. Look at her. Isn't she beautiful …"

Those were King Lear's last words. With a sigh, he fell forwards across her body and joined her in death.

"Oh, my king," cried Kent, sobbing into his hands.

"But Britain must have a ruler," said Albany. He looked around at Edgar, son of the Duke of Gloucester, and the Earl of Kent. "All the king's family are dead, and Cornwall and the Duke of Gloucester and Edmund, too. We're the only three nobles left and I'll not take the throne."

"Nor I," sobbed Kent.

"Then it must be you," said Albany to Edgar.

Edgar nodded. "I can't be happy to take a crown amongst all this death but it's my duty, and I'll serve Britain as I must."

And that, my friends, is how Edgar became King of Britain. It's a sad story, and a warning. The country's heart was broken for the sake of money and jewels and land and the power to order people around. There's no happy ending, no joke that I can make that'll bring back all the soldiers who died for Regan and Goneril's jealousy and greed. But there's a little hope, too. As long as there are good, kind people, like Edgar, then perhaps wickedness will never truly win.

Families at war

Ideas for reading

Written by Clare Dowdall, PhD
Lecturer and Primary Literacy Consultant

Reading objectives:
- identify and discuss themes and conventions in and across a wide range of writing
- prepare poems and plays to read aloud and to perform, showing understanding through intonation, tone and volume so that the meaning is clear to an audience
- predict what might happen from details stated and implied

Spoken language objectives:
- gain, maintain and monitor the interest of the listener(s)

Curriculum links: PSHE

Resources: drawing materials; joke books

Build a context for reading

- Look at the image on the front cover. Ask children who they think the portrait shows, and what they think the story might be about. Explain that *King Lear* is a famous tragedy by William Shakespeare.
- Turn to the blurb. Read it together and establish who is who. Reread the blurb, using separate voices to emphasise the characters' feelings and motives.
- Turn to pp2-3. Help children to read each character's name and description.

Understand and apply reading strategies

- Ask children to read Chapter 1 quietly, noting the key information in the plot.
- Help children to recount the key information as a group, and create a flow chart on a whiteboard, checking children's understanding of the events.